Happy Easter, Dear Dragon

by Margaret Hillert
Illustrated by Jack Pullan

NORWOODHOUSE PRESS

DEAR CAREGIVER,

The books in this Beginning-to-Read collection may look somewhat familiar in that the original versions could have been a part of your own early reading experiences. These carefully written texts feature common sight words to provide your child multiple exposures to the words appearing most frequently in written text. These new versions have been updated and the engaging illustrations are highly appealing to a contemporary audience of young readers.

Begin by reading the story to your child, followed by letting him or her read familiar words and soon your child will be able to read the story independently. At each step of the way, be sure to praise your reader's efforts to build his or her confidence as an independent reader. Discuss the pictures and encourage your child to make connections between the story and his or her own life. At the end of the story, you will find reading activities and a word list that will help your child practice and strengthen beginning reading skills. These activities, along with the comprehension questions are aligned to current standards, so reading efforts at home will directly support the instructional goals in the classroom.

Above all, the most important part of the reading experience is to have fun and enjoy it!

Shannon Cannon

Shannon Cannon,
Literacy Consultant

Norwood House Press • www.norwoodhousepress.com
Beginning-to-Read™ is a registered trademark of Norwood House Press. Illustration and cover design copyright ©2017 by Norwood House Press. All Rights Reserved.

Authorized adapted reprint from the U.S. English language edition, entitled Happy Easter, Dear Dragon by Margaret Hillert. Copyright © 2017 Margaret Hillert. Reprinted with permission. All rights reserved. Pearson and Happy Easter, Dear Dragon are trademarks, in the US and/or other countries, of Pearson Education, Inc. or its affiliates. This publication is protected by copyright, and prior permission to re-use in any way in any format is required by both Norwood House Press and Pearson Education. This book is authorized in the United States for use in schools and public libraries.

Paperback ISBN: 978-1-60357-881-3
The Library of Congress has cataloged the hardcover edition of this book with the following call number: 2015046741

This book was manufactured as a paperback edition. If you are purchasing this book as a rebound hardcover or without any cover, the publisher and any licensors' rights are being violated.

297R-092016
Printed in ShenZhen, Guangdong, China.

Oh, my.
Oh, my.
Come out here.
Look at this—
        and this—
        and this!

3

What pretty ones.
See here, and here, and here.
Red, yellow, and blue ones.

I can make something.
Something for you.
It is pretty.
Do you like it?

Now come with me.
Run, run, run!
I want you to see something.

Look here.
Look here.
Look at the little yellow balls.
Look at the little yellow babies.

Come, look here.
Look down in here.
Little babies are here, too.

And see this.
One, two, three babies.
I like the little babies.

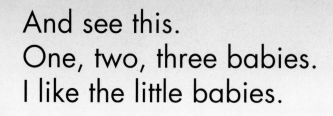

Oh, oh.
What is this?
See it come down.
Run, run, run!

Look at that.
Do you see what I see?
It is pretty.
We can make something pretty too.

Mother, Mother.
We want to do something.
Can you guess what?
Can you help us?

Yes, yes.
I can guess what you want.
And I can help.

Look here.
Here is what you want.
Now get to work.
You and Father get to work.
Work, work, work.

Oh, my.
How pretty!
What good work you do.

You can do this, too.
Come and do this.
You will have to work at it.

That is good.
It is pretty.
I like it.

Now Mother has something.
Something for us.
We have to find it.
We have to go and look for it.

Oh, Mother.
Here it is.
And it is good to eat, too.

Look at us now.
We look good.
It is fun to do this.

I will go in here.
You can not come in.
But do not go away.
I will come out.

We can go now.
Here you are with me.
And here I am with you.
Oh, what a happy Easter,
Dear Dragon.

The following activities support the findings of the National Reading Panel that determined the most effective components for reading instruction are: Phonemic Awareness, Phonics, Vocabulary, Fluency, and Text Comprehension.

Phonemic Awareness: The long e sound

Oddity Task: Say the long **e** (as in Easter) sound for your child. Ask your child to find and say any word that has the long **e** sound in the following word groups:

bee, bet, bin	man, mean, mom	dear, dirt, dart
fun, fan, funny	tent, top, tree	salt, seal, sent
hip, hop, happy	red, read, road	

Phonics: The letter Ee

1. Demonstrate how to form the letters **E** and **e** for your child.
2. Have your child practice writing **E** and **e** at least three times each.
3. Ask your child to point to the words in the book that have the letter **e** in them.
4. Write the words listed below on separate pieces of paper. Read each word aloud and ask your child to repeat them.

dear	happy	Easter	family	baby
three	eat	pretty	read	meet
sleep	seat	silly	jeep	meat

5. Write the following long **e** spellings at the top of a piece of paper.

   ee   ea   y

6. Ask your child to sort the words by placing them under the correct long **e** spelling.

Vocabulary: Story Words

1. Write the following words on separate pieces of paper and point to them as you read them to your child:

flowers	chicks	ducklings	babies
eggs	hunt	basket	raindrops

2. Say the following sentences aloud and ask your child to point to the word that is described:

- In the springtime, these plants bloom in pretty colors. (flowers)
- These fall from the sky to help plants grow. (raindrops)
- Spring is when many animals have their (babies).
- Baby chickens are called (chicks).
- Baby ducks are called (ducklings).
- For Easter, we dye these in many different colors (eggs).
- When you go looking for hidden eggs it is called an Easter egg (hunt).
- When you find eggs on an Easter egg hunt, you can put them in a (basket).

Fluency: Echo Reading

1. Reread the story to your child at least two more times while your child tracks the print by running a finger under the words as they are read. Ask your child to read the words he or she knows with you.

2. Reread the story, stopping after each sentence or page to allow your child to read (echo) what you have read. Repeat echo reading and let your child take the lead.

Text Comprehension: Discussion Time

1. Ask your child to retell the sequence of events in the story.

2. To check comprehension, ask your child the following questions:

- After it rained, what happened when the sun came out?
- What do you think the people on page 24 and 25 are doing?
- If your family celebrates Easter, ask: What do we do to celebrate Easter?
- If your family does not celebrate Easter, ask: What special celebrations do we have in the spring? What do we do to celebrate?

WORD LIST

Happy Easter, Dear Dragon uses the 70 words listed below.

This list can be used to practice reading the words that appear in the text. You may wish to write the words on index cards and use them to help your child build automatic word recognition. Regular practice with these words will enhance your child's fluency in reading connected text.

a	Easter	I	oh	us
am	eat	in	one(s)	
and		is	out	want
are	Father	it		we
at	find		pretty	what
away	for	like		will
	fun	little	red	with
babies		look	run	work
balls	get			
blue	go	make	see	yellow
but	good	me	something	yes
	guess	Mother		you
can		my	that	
come	happy		the	
	have	not	this	
dear	has	now	three	
do	help		to	
down	here		too	
dragon	how		two	

ABOUT THE AUTHOR Margaret Hillert has helped millions of children all over the world learn to read independently. She was a first grade teacher for 34 years and during that time started writing books that her students could both gain confidence in reading and enjoy. She wrote well over 100 books for children just learning to read. As a child, she enjoyed writing poetry and continued her poetic writings as an adult for both children and adults.

Photograph by Glenna Washburn

ABOUT THE ILLUSTRATOR A talented and creative illustrator, Jack Pullan, is a graduate of William Jewell College. He has also studied informally at Oxford University and the Kansas City Art Institute. He was mentored by the renowned watercolor artists, Jim Hamil and Bill Amend. Jack's work has graced the pages of many enjoyable children's books, various educational materials, cartoon strips, as well as many greeting cards. Jack currently resides in Kansas.